For Dave, Tina and Esther (2 Cor. 5:17)

The White BICYCLE

written and illustrated by
Rob Lewis

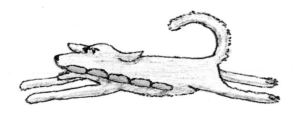

Macdonald

Mum was fed up because the garage was in such a mess. She decided it was time to clear out the rubbish.

'You don't need your old bike any more,' Mum said to Ravi. 'It's rusty and dirty.'

Dad took the bike to a rubbish dump
and threw it into the nettles with all the
other junk. Ravi didn't mind too much.
After all, the bike *was* rusty and dirty.

A tramp was passing by and saw the bike.
'Just what I need!' he said. He brushed it
off and rode off down the lane.

The tramp overslept the next morning,
and while he was dozing a runner came along
and saw the bike.
'Just what I need,' he said.
'Now I can win the race!'

But the runner pedalled so fast
that he rode over a stone.
He went flying through the air –

and landed in a pile of hay.

When it was dark, a poacher
stealing fish from the river
saw the bike.
'Just what I need!' he said.

He put the fish in the basket,
fixed his lamp to the front,
and rode off into the night.

But as he pedalled up the lane,
the poacher saw the gamekeeper!
He was so scared that he left
the bike and the fish behind,
and ran off across the fields.

Later that night, two people were coming
home from a party and saw the bike.
'Just what we need!' they said, and they
both climbed on to the bike.
They wobbled off down the road until
they came to a steep hill, and went
so fast that . . .

they went off the road, through a gate,
across a field and over a tent.
The campers were not very pleased.

As the sun came up, Mrs Simpson began her long walk to the town to do her shopping. 'Just what I need!' she said when she saw the bike left in the field. She got on the bike and cycled to town.

Mrs Simpson left the bike outside
Joe's Junk shop and went shopping.
When Joe saw the bike, he thought
it had been left for him to sell.

Joe took the bike into his workshop
and cleaned it up.

Then he painted it white to make
it look smart.
'Just what I need to brighten up the shop!'
said Joe. 'I'll put it in the best place,
right at the front.'

Ravi saw the gleaming white bicycle outside the shop.

'Mum, can I have that lovely bike, please?'
he asked.
'Okay,' said Mum.

Ravi was pleased with his new bike.
It was rather like his old one!

Other picture books by Rob Lewis published by Macdonald
Hello Mr Scarecrow
The Great Granny Robbery
Friska the Sheep that was Too Small

A MACDONALD BOOK

© Rob Lewis 1988

First published in Great Britain in 1988
by Macdonald & Co (Publishers) Ltd
London & Sydney
A member of Maxwell Pergamon
Publishing Corporation plc

Printed and bound in Spain
by Cronion S.A.

Main text set in Optima Bold educational face.

Macdonald & Co (Publishers) Ltd
Greater London House
Hampstead Road
London NW1 7QX

British Library Cataloguing in Publication Data

Lewis, Rob, 1962–
    The white bicycle.
    I. Title
    823'.914[J]   PZ7

    ISBN 0–356–13794–5
    ISBN 0–356–13795–3 Pbk